What Kids Say About
Carole Marsh Mysteries . . .

I love the real locations! Reading the book always makes me want to go and visit them all on our next family vacation. My Mom says maybe, but I can't wait!

One day, I want to be a real kid in one of Ms. Marsh's mystery books. I think it would be fun, and I think I am a real character anyway. I filled out the application and sent it in and am keeping my fingers crossed!

History was not my favorite subject till I starting reading Carole Marsh Mysteries. Ms. Marsh really brings history to life. Also, she leaves room for the scary and fun.

I think Christina is so smart and brave. She is lucky to be in the mystery books because she gets to go to a lot of places. I always wonder just how much of the book is true and what is made up. Trying to figure that out is fun!

Grant is cool and funny! He makes me laugh a lot!!

I like that there are boys and girls in the story of different ages. Some mysteries I outgrow, but I can always find a favorite character to identify with in these books.

They are scary, but not too scary. They are funny. I learn a lot. There is always food which makes me hungry. I feel like I am there.

What Parents and Teachers Say About Carole Marsh Mysteries . . .

I think kids love these books because they have such a wealth of detail. I know I learn a lot reading them! It's an engaging way to look at the history of any place or event. I always say I'm only going to read one chapter to the kids, but that never happens—it's always two or three, at least!
—Librarian

Reading the mystery and going on the field trip—Scavenger Hunt in hand—was the most fun our class ever had! It really brought the place and its history to life. They loved the real kids characters and all the humor. I loved seeing them learn that reading is an experience to enjoy!
 —4th grade teacher

Carole Marsh is really on to something with these unique mysteries. They are so clever; kids want to read them all. The Teacher's Guides are chock full of activities, recipes, and additional fascinating information. My kids thought I was an expert on the subject—and with this tool, I felt like it!
—3rd grade teacher

My students loved writing their own Real Kids/Real Places mystery book! Ms. Marsh's reproducible guidelines are a real jewel. They learned about copyright and more & ended up with their own book they were so proud of!
 —Reading/Writing Teacher

"The kids seem very realistic—my children seemed to relate to the characters. Also, it is educational by expanding their knowledge about the famous places in the books."

"They are what children like: mysteries and adventures with children they can relate to."

"Encourages reading for pleasure."

"This series is great. It can be used for reluctant readers, and as a history supplement."

The Ghosts of
Pickp_cket
Plantation

by Carole Marsh

Managing Editor: Sherry Moss
Cover Design: Michele Winkelman
Illustrations: Brittany Donaldson, Savannah College of Art & Design
Content Design: Steven St. Laurent, Line Creek Creative

Gallopade is proud to be a member and supporter of these educational
organizations and associations:

American Booksellers Association
International Reading Association
National Association for Gifted Children
The National School Supply and Equipment Association
The National Council for the Social Studies
Museum Store Association
Association of Partners for Public Lands

a Word from the author

Dear Reader,

My granddaughter, Christina, and I like to speculate on "What if?"
As you may know, I write mysteries set in real places that feature real
kids as characters. The story is made up (fiction), but the fascinating
historic facts are true (non-fiction). We are often amused when
readers guess "backwards" about what I made up and what is true in
the books. Sometimes I have a hard time being sure myself! Why?
Because history is just as interesting and incredible as anything an
author can make up.

So, one day, Christina and I were wondering: "What if a boy who
had no parents, or hopes of ever having a real family, went to stay on
a spooky (maybe haunted?) old rice plantation with an aunt who was
a lawyer in Savannah? It was easy to imagine a story that could be
interesting, funny, scary, and feel real. But the truth is, Savannah,
Georgia, has so much flabbergasting history that you have a big head
start on a great story, no matter what you write about!

As I told Christina about the real General Edward Oglethorpe...
the Indians Mary Musgrove and Tomochichi...the quirky characters
who live in Savannah today...the sad past of slavery and the Civil
War...and how I have to keep an eye out for giant "gators" when I play
golf on coastal courses...well it all seemed Pretty Darn Scary. I hope
you, and Christina, think so, too!

Carole Marsh
Savannah, Georgia

Pretty Darn Scary Books in This Series

the ghosts of Pickpocket Plantation

the Secret of Skullcracker Swamp

the Phantom of thunderbolt fort

the Secret of Eyesocket Island

table of Contents

Preface

a Place Called Pickpocket

The place called Pickpocket Plantation is fictional, perhaps. If that is intriguing to you, then consider how intriguing it is to me to make up a place that, perhaps, after all, exists! It does not matter whether it actually did or did not for the purpose of this story.

Here's why:

Pickpocket Plantation, in my story, is located on the Savannah River near the Georgia-South Carolina border. Many plantations were once located in this area. Those in coastal Georgia are largely now ruins, or less. Some in South Carolina still exist, especially those tucked between the Ashepoo, Combahee, and Edisto Rivers. In fact, an archipelago of plantations once trickled down the eastern seaboard from Virginia to Florida.

But this story is not so much about a dot on a map or a place, as it is about a point in time, or perhaps...points in time. If that sounds like the proverbial riddle inside a puzzle inside an enigma, it is. Riddles intrigue us, confound us, and tease us to press on to try to unsnarl fact from fiction, not always an easy thing.

Pickpocket, like many of the plantations I have alluded to, existed in a semi-watery wetland reigned over by ancient oaks that seemed ageless and enormous, even as youths. They loomed (and still loom) over these sites like sentinels, having seen all, continuing to see all. It probably matters not to them whether the Terry in my story is from the past, present, or future. What is time when you are ageless? Another riddle.

Much of the detail in the story is drawn from places I have seen, visited, and by day or by night, found pretty darn scary. Why scary? I cannot say. Perhaps because when I am at the coordinates of a former place of home, family, birth, death, struggle, survival, and more, I feel that I am standing in a place called History. Not the history of boring textbooks, but history that lived and breathed, and still lives and breathes, watching, waiting... like the giant gray-bearded trees...for what comes next.

What comes next, in these chapters, is Terry's experience. But one day, if you can, you yourself might go and visit a former plantation site, named Pickpocket or something equally quaint, and see what you discover.

What I have discovered visiting such places (and reading about the people and events that took place there) is that even in the apparently remote outpost, every place is a crossroads, and history happens just as surely as the wind blows. "You came and wrote about our place, and after you left some of the things you said that you made up actually came to pass," the director of a plantation historic site once told me. "Are you complaining?" I asked, as if I had any control over what happened in the dark at distant places. "No," he said, "only marveling at how mysterious it all is. Sometimes, even scary."

Things do go bump in the night, but sometimes it's just grandpa's toppling shoe, and other times? Well, I'm sure I can't say...can you?

Carole Marsh
Savannah, Georgia
Summer 2006

Chapter One

his name was telesphore

HIS NAME WAS TELESPHORE. He had no idea why his grandmother had named him that. His grandmother had had to name him because his mother had died giving birth to him. His father was nowhere to be found. No name had been selected, not even hinted at, much less batted about from some charming book of baby names. So his grandmother named him Telesphore. Thank goodness his friends called him Terry. But somehow, deep underneath, he felt like Telesphore, a name that seemed auspicious, but also a burden. But he couldn't think of that now. Now he had to think of snakes.

Water moccasins were part and parcel of the peat bog swamp that surrounded Pickpocket Plantation. So were alligators. Mosquitoes the size of saucers. Wild turkeys. And, rarely, a wild boar.

"Watch where you s.....t......e......p," Terry reminded himself. His Aunt Penelope had lent him a beat-up old pair of hightop, lace-up boots, but he figured a diamondback rattler's fangs could easily pierce right through the leather as if it were butter. Terry realized that he had involuntarily squiggled his feet so far back up into his shoes that his toes were cramping. "Step carefully," he whispered to himself.

Terry wondered how anyone had ever gotten anything done going tippy-toe around the enormous plantation acreage. "Shoot," he said aloud, again to himself, "I will just stomp along like brave Huck Finn might have done and take what comes." As he walked more willfully, he tried to recall if Tom Sawyer and Huck Finn had been more brave, or cowardly. Either way, they were on the Mississippi River, and Terry did not think alligators the length of small cars had ever worried them, except perhaps in their imaginations.

In Terry's imagination, he was scouting out Pickpocket as it must have been in the days of the Yamacraw Indians, or in the painful era of plantation slavery, or during the wily time of the Civil War (the War of Northern Aggression, as some old-time southerners still called it), or some other time of historic excitement. But, really, Terry knew in his heart that he was just trying not to be bored.

Or scared. After all, didn't Aunt Penelope say that the Saturday *Savannah Pilot* recently featured a story about a fisherman poling his skiff through some snarled morass of wetland weeds getting his foot chomped off by a gator?

"Step carefully, Terry...

c   a   r   e   f   u   l   l   y."

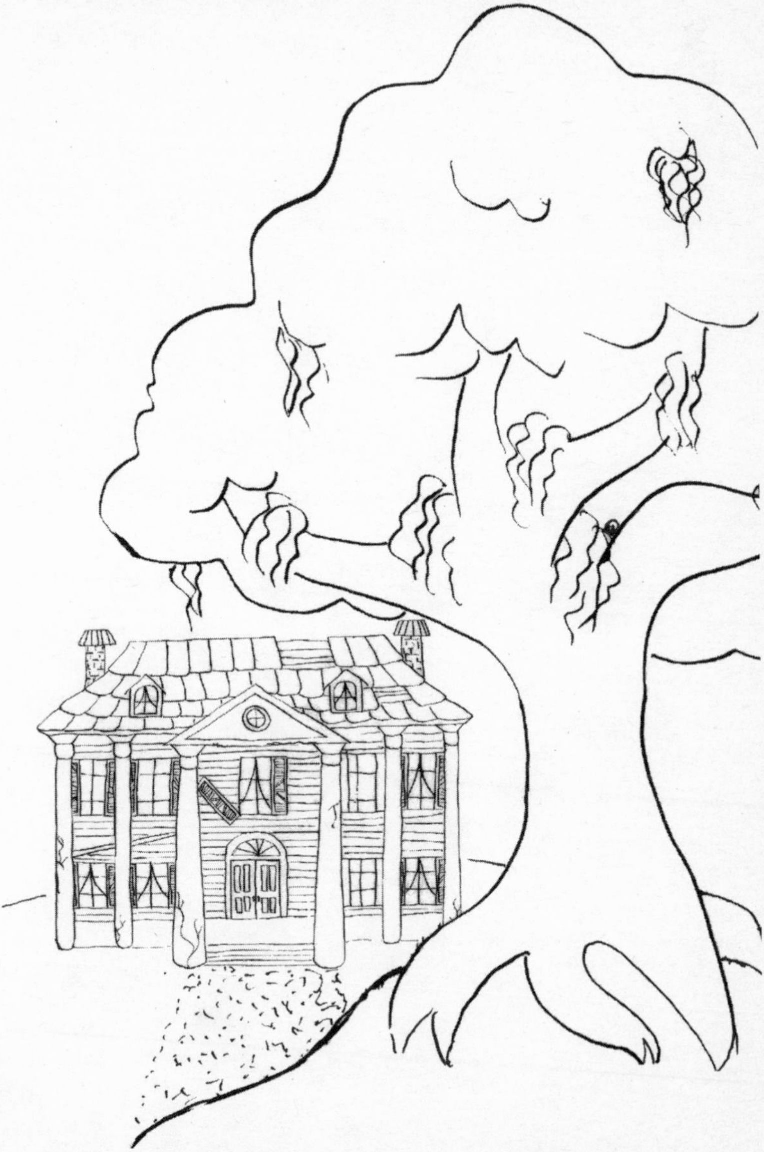

Chapter two

aunt Penelope

"I hate to leave you overnight again, Terry," the smartly-dressed woman said. "I feel so guilty. Maybe we can work out something better, soon. We're in the middle of all these gnarly negotiations and I have to be on the corporate jet by seven. We won't be back until late. I'll try to get you a cell phone today, at the least. Promise, big guy!"

Terry's aunt, Penelope Purser, called Pen by her fellow lawyers for her great writ-writing skills, stood in the doorway of the big plantation house and grinned at him sadly. For every degree she was cool—even if she was almost forty years old—Terry was, in his mind, quadruple degrees uncool.

His Aunt Penny swung her worn leather "lucky" briefcase nervously. She looked like she felt terrible about leaving him, but she looked even more nervous about missing that flight—though how she could when it was still dark outside and the Savannah-Hilton Head

International Airport was only a few miles away, he had
no idea.

Terry shrugged. "It's OK, Aunt Pen, really. I'll be
OK. Promise right back at you." He gave her a goofy
grin to get her to believe him. He hated to spend yet
another day alone at the old plantation, but it wasn't her
fault that he was here. Mostly, right now, he was sleepy
and wanted to go back to bed.

His aunt sighed. "Gee, Terry, it'll be the weekend
soon and I'll take you to Savannah. We'll do something
fun, promise."

Promises. Definition: things to be broken. "Sure,"
Terry said, agreeably. "Better go; they can't win the
case if you miss the plane."

Aunt Penny snapped her fingers with her free hand,
as if her nephew had just had a brilliant idea. "Right!"
With the same hand, she blew him a kiss across the wide
entranceway to where Terry stood propped against the
door to the parlor. "Step carefully!" she said merrily,
her ever-constant reminder to him. Then she spun on
her high heels and charged down the steps to the *beep-
beep* of her car's auto lock.

When the headlights flashed on, they illuminated a
ghostly streak through the dark oak forest. With a final
wave and a soft rustle of leaves and pinestraw, his aunt
was gone, the evil red eye dots of the tail lights winking
as she sped down the lane until they disappeared into
the darkness.

Chapter three

home alone

Home Alone, thought Terry, as he shuffled back up the soaring staircase to his second-floor bedroom. Although his aunt had offered him any of the larger extra bedrooms in the house, he had chosen this small one in a far corner under the eaves. It had twin beds and he liked pretending that perhaps an older brother might come flouncing into the room, all hot and sweaty after an all-out basketball practice, and flop down and say, "Hey, bro, where ya been? Thought you might come by the gym. Missed ya, big guy." He would sling a sweaty towel at Terry and with a teasing grin say, "C'mon, we'll go get tacos with the gang."

Terry crawled back beneath the faded coverlet on the bed. Aunt Penny called it a counterpane. He thought it was just an old quilt, once beautiful, but now shabby-edged and yet worn so soft it felt like cool grandma cheek skin beneath his hand. He thought of that analogy because at the orphanage, one of the volunteer houseparents had been a grandmother with pale white skin that felt like wet silk when she gave goodbye hugs and kisses. Gee, he thought, snuggling deep beneath the covers, that must have been when I was just two or three...

Home Alone was never the truth back then. After his own grandmother had passed away, he had gone to live at the Methodist Children's Home in Decatur. If he had any other family no one had found them, except Aunt Penny, and she was in Europe studying legal history at some university in England on a scholarship. No one had even bothered to contact her.

An orphanage is an orphanage; you can't change the facts of why you are there. But the Home was good to him. Needless to say there were always a bunch of kids around, so actually, Terry realized, he was sort of enjoying this peace and quiet—only it was so peaceful and so quiet that it was creepy. He felt like he had been dropped off at the end of the world for the summer. His Aunt Penny had insisted he come. "Unless I ever get married, we're each other's only family," she had said. "It won't be long before you're thinking of college and since I'm making money now, I can help you."

"I can get a Hope Scholarship," Terry had told her. He was a good student and his schools had been good and the Decatur Public Library, just down the street from the Home, had been his second home.

Terry wasn't even sure he wanted to go to college. He knew he was smart, smart enough to know that some famous guys who had gotten to be billionaires, like Bill Gates of Microsoft Computer, not to mention Apple's Steve Jobs, and Dell's whatever-that-guy's-name was, had NOT gone to college. He wondered if they were just brilliant? In too big a hurry to do what they wanted to wait on college? Too bored? Stubborn? He wished he could ask them.

Terry, himself, knew that antsy tug to "do something," only what that something was he didn't know. He guessed that he would figure it out someday. He liked physics a lot, archaeology a little, and astronomy was OK. But what did that mean he should do, or study? How, he always wondered, was he going to finally leave the Home, like the proverbial baby chick from the nest, and make his way in life? He wanted to travel and have a good job and make some money. Maybe help kids who had grown up like him. But mostly, he wanted his own family. Right now, all that seemed like a dream. Very possibly, an impossible dream.

What also seemed like a dream was the *crunch crunch crunch* of footsteps on dry leaves outside the house, just beneath his bedroom window. The very earliest dawn light was beginning to creep across the forest floor. Terry jumped up and looked out the

window just in time to see a black man entering the side
door to the kitchen.

Chapter four

nus Marster

There were two staircases in the house. One was a grand wishbone-shaped staircase that led to the entry hall and front door. The other was a twisting, narrow staircase that took you directly into the kitchen. From his bedroom Terry could get to either and he wondered which to take.

His heart racing, he tiptoed one step at a time down the back staircase. His goal of stealth and silence was futile. Each step creaked, groaned, or moaned. Sweat formed on his brow. He was expecting no one. Aunt Penny had not mentioned any workman or anyone else coming out to the house today, though Lord knows it needed work, lots of work.

All Terry knew was that he had no choice but to check on the brazen stranger who had entered the house. If he had passed on through to some of the other downstairs rooms, then he probably would not hear Terry's creaking footsteps. But when he reached the bottom landing and stepped into the kitchen, the man was sitting at the table, humming softly as he worked at cracking and picking a scattered stack of large black walnuts.

He did not even look up. Terry cleared his throat softly, then louder. When the man still did not look up, Terry, exasperated though still scared, stepped forward. With his hands on the hips of his pajama bottoms, he said as masterfully as he could, "Sir?"

"Yah, boy, set down," the old man said. His voice, as deep and mournful as a foghorn, rolled like thunder through the kitchen. Yet he was still concentrating on his task as he spoke.

Terry inched forward and pulled out a chair. He figured the only way the man was going to communicate was if he sat down and got in his face.

"Wan' taste?" the man asked, thrusting a perfect black walnut half into Terry's startled face. Terry didn't know what else to do so he accepted the offer and stuffed the nut in his mouth; it was delicious.

"Got get dis done," the man said. "Dis cake-bakin' day. Miz Annadale be angry by me iffn I not done by the time she gets ready to mix batter."

Terry swallowed and cleared his throat again. "Sir," he repeated, "who are you?"

Now the old man looked up, ratcheted his neck forward and stared the boy in the eye. "Why I Nus Marster, boy. Who you think I am?" He offered another walnut half, again, perfectly picked out like a miniature work of art.

Terry thought about that for awhile. No answer on earth came to him.

Chapter five

the Walnut Man

In the spreading morning light, Terry silently studied the busy old man and thought just how much his gnarled face resembled the meat inside those black walnut shells. It was a face of great age, hard word, grave dignity, and concentration so dire you would have thought that walnut cracking and picking was as urgent and important as triage in an emergency room.

The buttery morning sunlight accentuated the wrinkles and folds in the cocoa-colored skin. The tight gray close-cropped hair and watery brown eyes gave the elderly man the look of having just walked out of a history book. Terry was still concerned why the man was sitting in his aunt's kitchen.

"Are you lost?" Terry asked before he realized that he had spoken his question aloud.

Again, the pumped-neck glare. "I ain't lost, boy. You lost? I speck I don't remember you." A bony brown finger pointed toward outdoors. "I came from Grave's

End like always do. Miss Annadale, she specks me and I be here. Get these nuts picked, go on to Miz Stiles; she be speckting me too. I Nus Marster, the nut man. You know who I is boy, don't mess with me here now."

The same bony finger shoved a nut across the table. This time it was an entire walnut expertly picked out of the shell. It looked a lot like a tiny tan brain. With surprise, Terry realized that it was almost too beautiful to eat.

"So you come each week?" Terry asked. He noted that the old man was all but skin and bones. His saggy brown pants were held up by faded suspenders over a worn shirt. A battered straw hat hung on the back of his chair.

Nus Marster continued to work, shaking his head back and forth at what he apparently deemed a very slow boy. "Course I come every week. They caint bake no nutcakes without me bringing the nuts, now can they." It was not a question. "I Nus Marster. I the walnut man," he added, just to be sure everything was clear. But to Terry, nothing was clear.

Suddenly the man's exasperation passed from his face and he looked up at Terry with a pleasant crook-tooth smile. "I knows you now. You dat boy whens you little I slip nuts in your pocket. You tell me you pick them out all day and wonder where they came from. You was just a little un then."

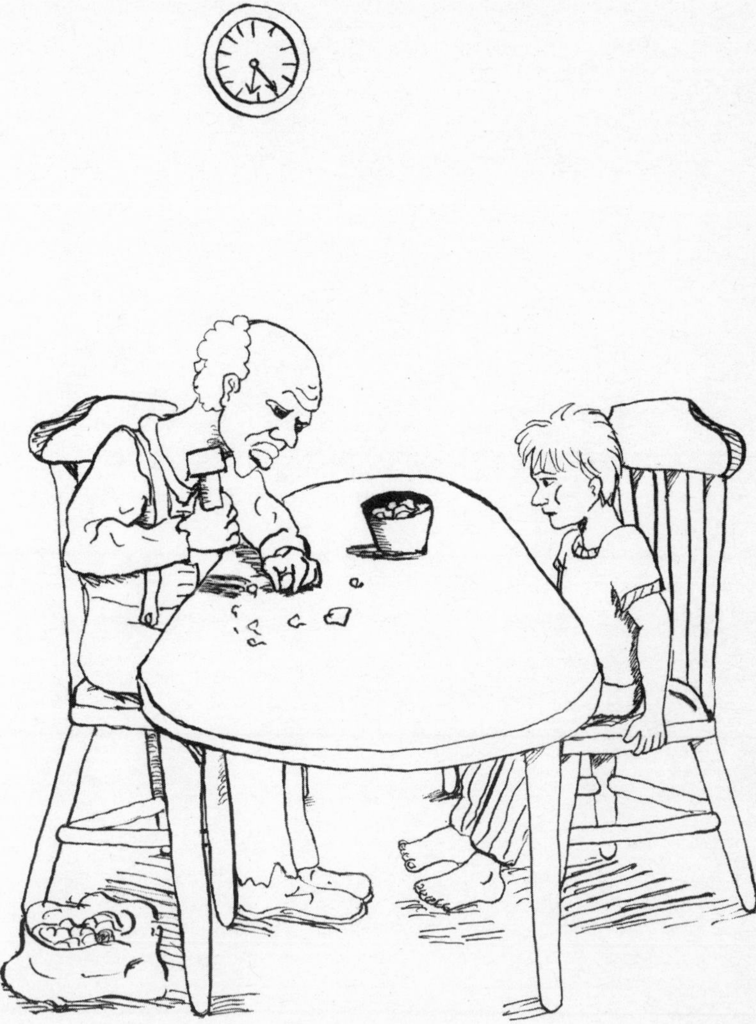

Just as quickly, the light of recognition faded from
the man's face. Without another word he brushed all
the walnut shells and other remains into the burlap sack
he had brought them in, dusted the table with his palm,
and patted the bowl of fresh-picked walnuts. "I take des
to the kitchen house now," he said, rising. "I bets old
Mae got the fire hot and the batter ready. She be fussin
me, I bets. She fuss, but she have a journeycake set
aside for my breakfast I 'magin."

Before Terry could stop him, the old man stood up
and started out the back door.

"But this *is* the kitchen," Terry said, not
understanding what was happening here so early in the
morning in his aunt's kitchen.

Nus Marster gave the boy another goofy grin and
shook his head. "Boy, you don't known nuthin. You
tryin to tease old Nus. The kitchen house be out back.
You knows dat."

The screen door slammed behind Nus Marster as
he headed out behind the plantation house. He
hummed as he moved quickly along, his gunnysack
tossed over his shoulder, the bowl of nuts held tightly
in the crook of his arm.

Terry scrambled to find his sneakers. As he yanked
them on he kept looking out the window, then back
down at his shoes to tie them, then out the window. By
the time Terry slammed out the back door, Nus Marster
was nowhere to be seen.

Chapter Six

the kitchen house

Terry stood in a pond of lime-gold sunlight. Long, pointed strands of Spanish moss festooned the brooding oak trees. A slight breeze blew the graybeards at an angle like a sail tacking to catch the wind. The only sound was the throaty moan of a distant rain crow.

Terry sat on the back stoop in the warm sun, which slowly settled the gooseflesh that had crawled out from under the short sleeves of his white tee shirt and snaked down his forearm. Just the chilly morning air, he reassured himself.

He thought of what Aunt Penny had told him when she had asked him to come and stay for the summer. She had been a young, hotshot lawyer in Atlanta earlier in her legal career. She had lived in a highrise condo in Buckhead, ran in the annual Peachtree Road Race marathon, and spent Saturday nights out with lawyer friends at neon-washed nightspots.

One day she had gotten a letter from a law firm in Savannah. Since she was not handling any jobs in that area, she had been surprised. Something, she said, about the expensive weathered gray paper and envelope with its almost cottonlike texture and a Spanish Moss watermark, had more than intrigued her. "It gave me goosebumps," she had confessed. "As if some voice from the past was whispering to me."

Terry had been fascinated. He had never had an adult share such intimate emotional information with him. It made him feel grown up to be entrusted with such heartfelt feelings, especially from someone he really didn't know all that well yet. It almost made him feel like he might be able to open up and share his feelings sometime. Just maybe...

Aunt Penny said she had opened the envelope carefully and had been almost startled to detect the faint, but pure and sweet, scent of Jessamine flowers escape from the envelope. But nothing was more surprising than what the letter—hand-written in a beautiful but masculine-strong hand in black ink—succinctly related.

THE LAW FIRM OF ABERCORN, HOLSHOUSER, PETTIGREW & ABLE
ONE LOWE STREET, SAVANNAH, GEORGIA

Dear Ms. Purser,

It is my duty to inform you that your distant relative, Ebidiah Oleander, passed away on St. Patrick's Day of this year. In a hand-written will, personally delivered to and held by our firm, Mr. Oleander bequeathed all his worldly possessions to you. Said possessions include the coastal plantation property [as noted by deed and plat attached] consisting of 678 acres and known as Pickpocket. A former rice plantation dating back to the 18th century, the property consists of said land, a plantation house, outbuildings, and other appendages.

At your earliest convenience, please contact our office to make arrangements to sign documents for the transfer of this property out of Mr. Oleander's estate. I regret that I am unable to tell you the condition of your property. Mr. Oleander was in a nursing home in South Carolina until his demise. I believe he entered that institution ten years ago, just after his visit to our firm to handle his Last Will and Testament.

With regards, your Friend and Etc.,

Justinian Habersham Abercorn, Esquire, of

The Law Firm: Abercorn, Holshouser, Pettigrew and Able
1 Lowe Street
Savannah, Georgia

Postscript: I understand you are a member of the Georgia Bar; please pardon my impertinence at relaying that our firm is seeking additional legal talent at this time.

As he recalled this earlier conversation with Aunt
Penny, Terry was surprised that he seemed to have
memorized the letter by heart, almost as if it had been
written to him. *Outbuildings*, he thought as he stood
there in the sun. He had not been here long enough to
explore anything but a little of the main house yet.
Could there be an outside kitchen? *A kitchen house?*

Terry peered at the snarl of brambles, kudzu vine,
and storm-toppled trees behind the house. It was the
direction that Nus Marster had headed. Terry rubbed
his arms briskly, then plunged into the woods.

Chapter Seven

Kudzu: the Vine that ate the South

As he put one foot in front of the other, Terry reminded himself to walk carefully. Aunt Penny had warned him that nature had pretty much taken over the plantation since its essential abandonment, "no telling how long ago."

The landscape behind the plantation house looked like something out of *The Secret Garden*, before the garden had been tamed. It was hard to see how Nus Marster had just walked off into this mess, Terry thought. There was no apparent path left from the past. Each step he took required a foot to stamp down undergrowth, a knee to shove thick vines aside, an elbow to nudge umbrellaed limbs upward, and a hand to protect his face from the backslap of leaves urgent to return to their status quo.

Soon he was inside a cave of brown and green. Sunlight barely penetrated. As thin bloody trickles appeared on his arms, Terry wished he had stopped to put on a long sleeve shirt to protect himself from thorns. Luckily, he had jeans to protect his legs.

It seemed quieter inside the thick overgrowth; no birds twittered. Any rustle caused Terry to jump. After all, it could be a twig, a snake, some small critter, an alligator, or something else he didn't want to think about or imagine at the moment. Running away from anything would be impossible since the forest snarl immediately closed back in behind him, as if he had never passed through.

He stopped for a moment to get his bearings when he heard something behind him. It was the tiniest *crick* of wood being trod upon, but to him it sounded like the breaking of a bone. He held his breath and stood perfectly still as pieces of forest moved behind him, shoved aside by what...he knew not.

In spite of himself, he gasped when a soft, wet *something* touched the back of his arm. Once. Again. Trembling, Terry turned to see a small fawn right behind him. When he moved, the fawn jumped, startled itself. Terry laughed.

"Tame little thing, aren't you?" he whispered softly to the fawn. It was so young, white spots clearly sprinkled its honey-colored back. The fawn twisted its head slightly then froze in place. "Your mama around?"

In answer, the fawn spun about and fled in slow motion as it hopped through the undergrowth. Ahead of it, Terry spied the white tail of a larger deer flash as if a flag of surrender. In a moment he could see neither of the animals and the forest was as quiet and lonesome as before.

Terry sighed and turned back to his task. After a few more deliberate steps, he reached out to brush aside a large mass of Spanish moss entangled with kudzu vine. Much to his surprise, he saw the faded red of old brick. Quickly, he yanked aside most of the greenery until he could see almost all of a side wall, part of a window, and the edge of a roof with the crumbled remains of a chimney sticking up into the only piece of blue sky he'd seen since he entered this part of the forest.

"The kitchen house!" he whispered.

Terry stood there a moment just thinking, regrouping his thoughts. *Careful*, he reminded himself. He twitched as he tugged a piece of Spanish moss off the back of his neck, wondering if ticks liked to nest in the gray lace. He thought he had learned in biology that Spanish moss was a parasite and a member, oddly enough, of the pineapple family. For extra measure, he brushed his neck again and shook at his shirt.

The kudzu was remarkable. Georgia, and many other southeastern states, were covered in it. Some people referred to the snaky green leaves as "the vine that ate the South." In fact, the plant could grow up to six inches in a single day. It was always weird to ride down the interstate and see the great expanses of trees and telephone poles, old tobacco barns, and other things not visible, covered over by the vine, creating thoughts of giant green monsters from the weird shapes it turned the ordinary landscape into.

"Kudzu, snakes, hmm," Terry coached himself aloud for comfort. "Ticks, gators, Nus Marster, what else?" The goosebumps were creeping back. So as not to be startled any more than necessary, Terry called loudly, "Nus? Nus! You here? You inside the kitchen house? It's just me, Terry."

It was only then that Terry put two thoughts together. One was that Nus had sworn he remembered Terry as a small boy. Impossible. But whomever he remembered, he insisted that he'd hidden walnuts in the boy's pocket and the boy picked them out to eat as he played around the plantation house.

"Could that be how *Pick...pocket* got its name?" he wondered aloud. With less bravery and more just to get it over with, Terry grabbed the old iron latch on the kitchen house door and shoved it wide open.

Chapter Eight

trickles of blood

A couple of field mice skittered away. Filtered light filled with sparkling dust motes spewed through a number of holes where bricks had fallen to the earth long ago. Except for a carpet of green kudzu tendrils that had insinuated their way into the building, the kitchen house appeared, to Terry, much as it might have a hundred years ago.

A large stone hearth supported a tangle of black andirons and other wrought iron paraphernalia used, he guessed, to prepare and cook food in the large brick fireplace. Old baskets hung on the wall, many with fist-sized holes popped through the woven straw. A black pot ("Surely large enough to call a cauldron?" Terry said aloud) stood akimbo to one side, one of its three legs crumbled into black dust.

More black pots lay around or hung from hooks on the walls. Many items, indeed, clung to the wall. Terry wasn't sure what might have been used for food

preparation or cooking or maybe washing or
candlemaking, or other necessary things he could not
think of at the moment.

A large table made of thick wooden planks stood to
one side, covered in a century of dust. In the corner, a
family of shabby pinestraw brooms of various sizes held
snarls of cobwebs. In fact, when Terry thought to look
up, he spied not only rafters, but a host of spiderwebs
overhead, hanging like silvery hammocks in the low light.

Terry brushed at his hair with the palm of one hand.
The one thing that he did not see was Nus Marster, nor
any sign of him. No nuts. No Miz Annadale or old Mae.
No scent of bread baking, not now, not in a very, very
long time.

Confused, disappointed, as well as thirsty and
hungry, Terry backed out of the house and gently tugged
the door closed. He dashed as quickly as the forest
allowed back toward the plantation house.

When he got inside the kitchen, Terry noticed that
blood still trickled in red squiggly signatures down his
arm. "I know Aunt Penny must keep iodine and
bandaids," he said aloud, wondering if this new thing of
talking to himself was going to continue. He could not
recall ever having talked to himself aloud in his life.

Sure enough, in the last kitchen cabinet he looked in
there was a clutter of paperwork, an old plantation

journal, and a much-rummaged through first aid kit. He used the dregs of a bottle of burgundy iodine and some mostly sticky bandaids to treat the worst scratches, then went to the sink to wash off the rest of the blood. It was a little creepy watching the swirls of dark red slither down the drain. It made him realize how bad it would be to truly get hurt out here all alone, an hour at least by dirt and gravel roads, to the main highway to Savannah. *Careful*, he thought again to himself.

Feeling better, Terry explored the cupboards. Aunt Penny mostly ate in town before she came home, so there was little food. "We'll shop this weekend," she had promised. However, there were plenty of old-fashioned dishes, most cracked, and all slightly dusty.

Terry was just filling a bowl with stale cereal when he heard the kitchen door creak open behind him. Whoever was entering the house expelled a great huff of air. When the door slammed behind him, along with a clatter of dropped and scattered who-knows-what, Terry spun around in fear.

He looked down to see Aunt Penny, still breathing hard, scrambling on the floor after items spilled from plastic grocery sacks. When she looked up, her nephew still stood there with a small silver spoon held aloft as if he were about to attack. It made her laugh.

"Scared you? Sorry," his aunt said.

"It isn't funny!" Terry said, embarrassed.

"Why didn't you holler or something? I wasn't expecting you till late tonight, you know." He tossed the spoon in the sink, suddenly with no appetite at all. In fact, he felt sort of sick to his stomach. Maybe he was coming down with something, he thought. Or maybe he was just homesick for the Home.

Finally, Terry came to his senses and dropped down to help his aunt with the many bags of food, paper towels, toilet paper, soft drinks, and other items she had bought in Savannah. The sight of some big, yellow bananas revived his appetite. He grabbed bag after bag from the floor and piled them on the countertop.

Aunt Penny touched his arm. "Are you OK?" she asked. "Did you hurt yourself?" She looked truly concerned and troubled. Terry felt bad for her. She was not used to worrying about anyone but herself. He knew she had no experience with kids and realized that he must be a really big nuisance and inconvenience.

He pulled his arm away. "I'm fine," he said, now embarrassed and aggravated. "I'm not six, you know. It's just some scratches I got outdoors earlier. I can't stay indoors all the time." Terry hung his head at his unforeseen and unwarranted outburst.

His aunt looked at him with guilt. "Sorry," she said. "I know that. I didn't mean that. Look, let's just start over." She paused. "How about some lunch, big guy?"

Terry laughed in spite of himself. "Sure," he said eagerly. "I'm absolutely starving."

Terry made big, fat peanut butter and jelly sandwiches, which he was shocked to find his aunt loved (maybe it was something in their genes?) just as much today as she had when she was his age. "The thicker the PB the better!" she hinted. He was delighted to see that she had bought thick-sliced white bread instead of that thin, whole-wheat stuff he saw the teachers at the Home nibble on. "And let's eat on the porch?" she asked as she headed upstairs to change clothes.

Terry nodded. He was not used to adults asking what he might want. By the time his aunt came back down in holey-kneed jeans and a stained white tee shirt, he had the sandwiches and big glasses of milk on the round metal table on the small screened porch.

"My kind of gourmet," Aunt Penny said, as she sat down. "Looks great!"

Terry blushed. "Thanks. But why are you home? I thought your flight left long ago?"

His aunt shook her head but she couldn't speak; she had a mouthful of sticky bread and peanut butter. With her hand she motioned for him to "hold on" as she chewed double-time so she could answer him. Finally she said, "Fog! Flight delayed, then cancelled. Everything got postponed until tomorrow. Sooooooo, I took the afternoon off to make sure my plantation prisoner didn't actually starve to death or have to resort to eating roadkill armadillo."

Once more, Terry laughed. His aunt was sort of old, but she was pretty cool and funny, he thought, especially when he imagined having to spend the summer with someone much, much older who maybe would treat him like a little kid. No, this wasn't great, but it wasn't too bad. He just had to settle in and get some routine down, and especially, quit jumping at every little creak and groan.

Thinking of that reminded him of Nus Marster, the walnut man. "You had a visitor today," Terry said. He was shocked to see his simple comment freeze his aunt's face into a mask of pure fear.

Chapter Nine

What Stranger?

Aunt Penelope grew angry. "Who!?"

"Hey," answered Terry. Her tone sounded so accusatory, he felt he had to defend himself. "It was just some old, black guy."

"Tall, right?" said Aunt Penny. She looked angrier than ever. "Thirtyish...big briefcase, silver car, fancy suit?"

Terry was stunned. "No," he assured her. "I mean it was an old black man, shabby, unkempt."

His aunt was unconvinced. "How old?"

Terry thought about it. Finally he said, "Old. Maybe even a hundred years old."

Now his aunt was silent. Suddenly she went from anger to concern. "Did he bother you? You didn't let him in, did you?"

"Whoa! Whoa!" cried Terry, crossing his arms in front of his face to protect himself from her onslaught. He laughed. "Harmless old dude, really, Aunt Penny...really."

She calmed down, but parallel lines wrinkled her brow. "Hmmmm...." she muttered, deep in thought.

Terry was confused. "What's up?" he said. "I don't get why you're so upset—first angry, then scared for me. Is there something I don't know?"

When his aunt laughed, Terry was at first offended. After all, he had been thrust into this place unprepared. He didn't know anyone. He didn't have a TV, phone, radio, bicycle, or any other form of communication or transportation. Maybe he was the one who should be angry or scared...or both, he thought. He realized that it was pretty darn scary out here, even in the daylight. He sure hoped that his aunt didn't plan on leaving him out here while she was away on any overnight business trips. No way!

Aunt Penny gently put her hand on her nephew's arm. "Terry, Terry," she said gently. "I'm sorry. I'm not laughing at you. I'm just chagrined at the stupid situation that I've gotten myself into." She shrugged and added. "I gotta laugh or I'll cry."

Terry was puzzled. He thought only kids got themselves into stupid situations. "Explain?" he asked hopefully.

His aunt sighed. "Eat," she said, pointing to his untouched sandwich. "I'll talk." She folded her arms across her chest and stared wistfully out the raggedy mesh screen to the forest.

"It's like this," she began. "After I got that letter from the lawyer about the will, I was all excited. I was tired of the big city, the rat race, the high costs, lots of things. Having an ancient colonial plantation fall into my lap seemed like some kind of serendipitous omen. I just *knew* I should move here, and without much thought, I did just that. Quit my job. Rented my condo. Moved. Took the job at the Savannah law firm. Lower pay, of course. Moved out here."

She said "moved out here" with a tremble in her voice. In fact, she pursed her lips as if she might indeed cry.

Terry nodded slightly, barely chewing; he didn't want to break the spell of her story.

His aunt continued. "I guess I had some dreams of making this a showplace, harking back to the olden days. Maybe have some friends down for long, luxurious weekends." To Terry's amazement, she hung her head and blushed. "Maybe even find me a handsome southern Savannah gentleman and get married. Have kids."

For a long while they were silent. A lonesome songbird *too-weeted* in a nearby oak. *Dreams.* That was something Terry knew about. Dreams thwarted. Dreams aborted. At last he asked, "Well?"

His aunt laughed loudly. "You're good for me, you know...just young enough to believe all things are possible, maybe even simple."

Terry didn't believe that at all, but he said nothing.

"It hasn't worked so well," his aunt went on. "I love the law firm and don't miss the big city life, but it's so lonesome out here. And, what's worse is that to truly fix this place up would cost a fortune. Make that a FORTUNE! No wonder so many of the old plantations are in ruins."

Then his aunt looked gravely serious. "But the worst thing is the developers. Down here, people know everybody's business. I guess some developers hoped that my uncle died intestate."

When Terry looked puzzled, his aunt giggled. "No, I didn't say 'died on the interstate,' I said *intestate*— without a will. Then they might have been able to get their claws on this land, which is actually in a great location—because of all the waterfront and being so close to Savannah—for an expensive housing development."

"You don't want to sell for a bunch of money?" Terry asked.

"Maybe someday," Aunt Penny confessed. "But I don't want to be *forced* into it."

"You sure did say *forced* forcefully," Terry noted. He wondered if that had anything to do with her concern about the stranger's visit today. "Who is the tall, black man with the cool car and fancy briefcase?"

His aunt frowned. "He's a developer's lawyer. Not a local developer nor a local lawyer, but smart aleck types from far away who think they can come down here to the Big, Dumb South and take us rednecks for suckers. And," she added, "they don't mind using strong-arm tactics, I hear."

Now Terry was beginning to understand. "So, you're saying you're scared of them?"

Too-weet...too-weet the birds chittered.

Aunt Penny said nothing.

Chapter ten

quilt girl

Two weeks later, Terry sat in a big armchair by a roaring fire in the large, gloomy parlor. Although he was no decorator-type, he could see why Aunt Penny thought this place could be beautiful.

On guard ever since his conversation with his aunt, Terry had explored the house more thoroughly and began to notice things. The rooms were many, large, and made even more airy and spacious-feeling with their high ceilings.

The many large windows hung from ceiling to floor and would have let in a great deal of cheerful sunlight, if all the overgrown bushes were trimmed away. The floors were wide slabs of beautifully-grained hardwood and they were put together with wooden pegs. In spite of the dimpled indentions made by the weight of heavy furniture and the scuffing and dust (Aunt Penny was no housekeeper!), Terry could tell that, if refinished, they would gleam like hot fudge.

Everywhere he looked, he began to notice details. Marble surrounds on the many fireplaces. Thick oak mantles. Cut glass chandeliers. Window glass as thick as dinner plates. Faded, but ornate, wallpaper. Heavy drapes that spilled onto the floor in rich, burgundy puddles. This had been no ordinary plantation, this has been a money-making operation, he thought.

By the fire, his imagination ran wild. Maybe pirate contraband had contributed to the fortunes of a former owner. Perhaps slaves who looked like Nus Marster had made the plantation master rich— working the land, then being sold to the highest bidder, once Georgia had finally relented and allowed slave trade in the reluctant colony.

The house's furnishings were another story. Like *Antiques Roadshow*, which he had sometimes watched on TV with an ailing foster mother, the house had an eclectic mix of probably valuable antiques sitting elbow-to-elbow with shabby chic from more recent eras. Terry figured the stupid lava lamp had been Aunt Penny's contribution to the mixed décor.

This afternoon, Terry hunkered down in an enormous armchair. Some of the stuffing poked out and was itchy, but the thick upholstery helped warm him on this chilly afternoon. He had been surprised how one day it could be hot and unbearably muggy...and the next, almost wintry when the sea breeze heaved in over the water and weaved through the shady forest.

Terry had come down with a stupid cold. Aunt Penny had brought him lots of cold pills, herbal teas, and thick socks and ordered him to "Stay put and read or something!" She seemed shocked at how a healthy young boy could turn into a snivelling sicko virtually overnight. "Get well!"

Actually, except for the cough and snuffy nose and watery eyes, Terry was sort of enjoying this unusual opportunity to camp out by a real wood fire and read, sip hot tea, and doze. Television would have been nice, but not any more dramatic than the old journal he was reading.

The scrawled calligraphy-like handwriting fascinated him. It was perfectly horrible to try to decipher. Had the journal-writer been sick? In a hurry? Each entry was brief and sounded so urgent.

Bad today.   The misery going around. Yellow fever!

Medicine not helping, too late.   Sassie died this morning.   House Joe tonight.

Babies.   Kids.

Flooding in the far fields... lost two mules.

Each entry seemed more dire than the next. Terry was surprised to read hardly a mention of anything good or fun. Not even any references to making a lot of money on crops. Indeed, it seemed that the crops were always too early, late, wet, dry, rotted, diseased, or something. He wondered why they bothered.

But it was the entries that mentioned the slaves that startled him most. Instead of any brutal, bossy words, the writer mostly added notes about trying to keep *Jessamine healthy*...or helping *deliver problem baby Nora*...or moving the *"darkies" to high ground before the Nor'easter hit*. Terry had found only one entry saying that a black had gone missing, but a subsequent entry proved he had not run off, but been *"taken" by a gator at the edge of the bay*. The thought made Terry shudder.

Suddenly, he felt a breeze like a ghostly hand pass through the room...indeed, across his lap, fluttering the bent corner of a journal page and ruffling the lace curtain. He froze.

"Laws, boy!" a voice screeched and Terry almost jumped out of his skin. He clutched the journal to his chest. His gasp caused him to cough raspily.

A young black girl with a wrap around her head, a peasant type blouse, and a striped skirt plopped down on the ottoman in front of him. All Terry could think was that if she were a ghost, she was much too close. *Much!*

The girl nonchalantly shoved his white socked feet over so she could get comfortable. She put her cocoa-colored face right up to his. "You looks sick as death, but not as purty," she said. Her voice was light and lilting and Terry could see that she was just a child. Nine? Ten? *But was she real?*

When the child thrust her palm against his forehead, Terry was startled but relieved to feel real skin instead of thin air. At least this ghost had form and substance.

"I thought I locked the doors," he whispered.

The girl laughed merrily. "No lock doors keep me out! I Missy. I got to get around. My job to clean the slops. Other piddlin' chores. I the house girl. You don' wan' me out, boy."

Missy grasped his teacup in her palm. "Dis cold, boy! I make you fresh tea. Add honey. You be better. Sit still. Hush that coughin'," she ordered and stood up.

As the girl scampered from the room, Terry looked around frantically. Could he escape? He stared at the tall windows, tightly closed, probably not opened in years. Was the girl alone? Was Nus Marster with her? Was this a trick? Who was she? What was going on? No wonder Aunt Penny had the heebie-jeebies living out here.

Before Terry could make any decision or draw any conclusion at all, Missy returned. Once more, she plopped back down in front of him and thrust a steaming cup of tea into his hand.

Terry sniffed the tea. "What's in this?" he asked, suspicious. Might she poison him?

Her response did nothing to reassure him. Missy gave him a crooked, dimpled grin and a wink. "Good stuff. Cure stuff. Drink it, boy."

The aromatic steam felt so good on his face. Terry took a sip. "Good," he admitted with a small nod. He thought it tasted like some magical combination of licorice and honey and something else—not liquor, he hoped. Not poison, he prayed.

Missy, looking extremely satisfied with herself, crossed her legs and reached into a large carpetbag she had tugged into the room. With a grunt, she pulled out a quilt. From the snow-white batting slipping out from between the sandwich of fabric, Terry could tell that it was a work in progress.

With a little hum, Missy reached back into the carpetbag and pulled out a small leather sack. It looked just like the sack Nus Marster had had with him.

"What's that?" Terry demanded.

"Notions, boy," Missy said with exasperation. She held up a spool of thread, a thimble, and a silvery needle. "I sew now."

And sew, she did. Terry watched, entranced, as the young child's hands expertly knotted thread, threaded needle, grasped fabric, and wove perfect tiny stitches in and out in time to her soft humming.

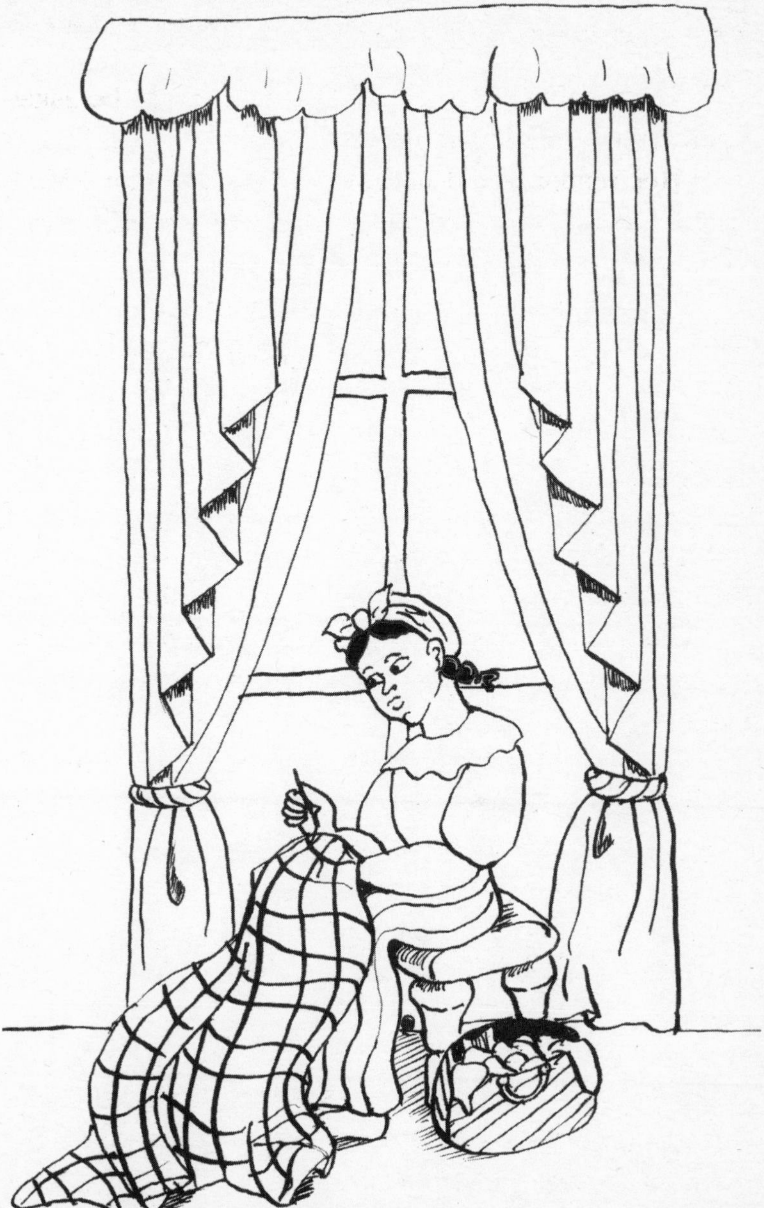

"How did you learn to sew?" Terry asked.

Missy looked at him like he was crazy in the head.

"Why, boy, my granny and my mama, o'course. What you think?" Missy pouted her lips in disgust. "You want to be warm? You better sew."

Missy donned a mischievous grin. She pulled her neck in like a little brown turtle and whispered. "If you want to hide a secret, you jes' might need a quilt!"

Terry was intrigued. Was the girl trying to tell him something? The tea, he guessed, was making him terribly drowsy. If he could keep her talking, he thought, she would be sitting right here when Aunt Penny came home from work. He glanced up at the grandfather clock; it was almost time...if she was on time, which rarely she was, but maybe he'd get lucky tonight. He didn't want her to think he'd made up another strange visitor.

"Tell me," he whispered back conspiratorially. "What secret? Do you have a secret?"

Without a word, Missy turned the quilt around and shifted one edge of it close to Terry's hand. When he just stared, puzzled, at the many small squares, Missy shook the fabric. When he finally spotted the peculiar square, he looked up at the girl and she nodded to him.

Terry reached out and felt the square. It was a patchwork piece of faded blue fabric. Three sides were sewn in tiny white stitches. But unlike the other completed squares, this square of fabric had one side left open. It formed a neat, all but imperceptible pocket.

"For secrets?" Terry guessed.

Missy nodded, a serious frown on her face.

"To keep hidden?" he added. She nodded.

Terry could see a small round bump in the center of the secret pocket square. He reached out his hand to feel the fabric to see if he could determine what Missy's hidden secret might be. Just as his hand touched the worn, silky fabric, the tea finally overtook him. He slumped down into the armchair in slumber, his hand falling to his side.

When he woke up, the blazing fire had turned to dusty white charcoal. The room was cold. His hand was cold. He had been dreaming about the secret pocket. *Pick...Pocket.* Could that be how the plantation had gotten its name?

Now jolted awake, Terry looked all around. Missy was gone, nowhere to be seen. In the kitchen, he could hear Aunt Penny grumbling to herself as she scrambled around preparing their late dinner.

Chapter Eleven

hidden Secrets

"Aunt Penny?" Terry said softly, so as not to startle her, as he entered the kitchen. She jumped anyway.

"Oh!" his aunt cried, nearly dropping the hot pan she held with a thick dishcloth. "Sorry. I'm still not used to having someone else in the house, I guess. Are you feeling better?"

Terry nodded. "Uh, sure," he said. "Some."

"Here, let me feel your head," his aunt insisted, heading toward him with an open palm. "Well, I think your fever has broken. Maybe you are on the mend," she added hopefully. Then she grinned like a foolish schoolkid. "I'm making you dinner!"

Terry slumped down into a kitchen chair and laughed/coughed. "Uh, I see..." He surveyed the kitchen which was now a mess, although he had to admit that the steamy air felt good on his face and the smells were promising. "I thought you didn't cook."

His aunt blushed. "Well, I don't, really. But I've always wanted to learn. Besides, the weather's gotten beastly out there tonight, and since you're sick and I'm starving I thought something homecooked would hit the spot." She plunked the blackened baking sheet she held with the dishcloth down on an iron trivet on the wooden table.

"Wow!" said Terry. "Homemade biscuits...I'm impressed." Just staring at them made his mouth water and his stomach rumble so loudly that it caused them both to laugh.

"Well, they won't get me on the Food Channel like Savannah's famous Paula Deen, but hopefully they taste all right," said Aunt Penny. "And since your stomach is out-booming the thunder, why don't you chow down on a couple while I finish the rest of dinner." She shoved a round of real butter and a pitcher of wildwood honey toward him.

Terry gave her no argument. He dug right in, splitting one of the funny-looking biscuits in half. He slathered it with the soft butter then drizzled honey over it and picked it up with both hands and bit down. "Gee," he said in earnest, "this is really delicious." The rest of his compliment was smothered in the wad of warm, sticky dough in his mouth.

If Aunt Penny had doubted his compliment, she was more than reassured by watching the hungry boy gobble down three more biscuits without saying a word. She poured him a large glass of milk so he wouldn't choke to death. *Poor boy*, she thought to herself. *He's starved for so many things.* But aloud she said, "Feed a cold, starve a fever, I guess."

In just a few minutes, she slapped down two plates loaded with thick fried pork chops, mounds of mashed potatoes, and a puddle of green peas. In addition, she poured a glistening brown gravy over the meat and potatoes. She made a glass of iced tea for herself, then sat down at the table.

"You, know," she said, with a teasing twinkle in her eye, "I've heard of growing boys, but now I've witnessed one in action!"

Terry gulped down his milk and gave her a 'Got milk?' grin. "Sorry," he said, not sorry at all. "I guess I was famished. And this looks like a feast, Aunt Penny—thanks for cooking tonight."

"You're welcome," his aunt said, truly delighted at the joy her nephew was finding in such a simple meal. "So, how was your day? Did you spend it right there by the fire?"

"Uh, yeah," Terry said. "I read the plantation journal some...it's real interesting. Buy why don't you tell me about your day...so I can...uh, eat?"

Aunt Penny laughed. "Sure, OK, if you want to hear a boring lawyer's day. Or is that a lawyer's boring day? Maybe both?"

Terry's mouth was already full, so he just gave her a shake of his head. He didn't think his aunt or her job were boring, what little he knew of her and her profession.

Aunt Penny took a deep breath and leaned forward, conspiratorially. She put her elbows on the table and tucked her fists up under her chin. "Well," she confessed, "I had a chance to work on a real live murder case today...or a real dead murder case is more accurate, I suppose. A woman is accused of murdering her much-younger husband. He was poisoned! Only, not with the usual stuff like arsenic or something, but with some wild-growing medicinal herb that he was probably allergic to. The problem is—which herb, and did she know he was allergic or not?!"

Fascinated, Terry just nodded and continued chewing. His aunt went on, "So I spent all day at the library researching things like dog fennel, black birch, and things like that. It seems that the Indians used to use this stuff all the time to treat illnesses from skin rashes to tummy aches. For example, black birch bark is filled with oil of wintergreen. You can brush your teeth with a twig, rub the oil on your skin to heal it, chew the leaves to soothe a funny belly, or drink tea made from the bark to treat a cold!"

"Or, poison your husband?" Terry said, spitting a fine dusting of flour in the air.

Aunt Penny grinned gleefully. "Possibly! Anyway, I learned that these woods—she waved her arm to indicate outdoors—are like a veritable pharmacy...IF you know what you're doing and chewing. Civil War-era doctors used tannins from blackberry roots to help clot blood from wounds. Even today, a lot of the old folks know all these so-called folk remedies, but you have to practice caution. Some plants are poison...especially if you're allergic to them."

"Wow," said Terry. "I didn't know lawyers got to do so many different things. That stuff is interesting."

Aunt Penny nodded. "Well, I think so. That's one thing that drew me to Pickpocket...all the fascinating history, legend, lore and mystery that surrounds—in fact, seems to seep from—a place that's been around so long. And this area's really special since it goes back to the time when Savannah was first founded. Heck, even before when the first native peoples lived here. I've heard there's an Indian midden on the plantation, but I haven't had time to scout it out yet, if I can even find it."

"A midden?" Terry asked, wondering if Aunt Penny had made desert.

His aunt pulled her plate toward her. "You know, a garbage heap...where the Indians would have tossed their refuse...oyster shells, bones, trash. Archeologists love to dig those up and see what was left behind. There may even be an Indian burial ground on the property! Wouldn't that be a hoot?"

Terry didn't answer. He hadn't really thought too much about all the history that had happened in this area. In the big city, things like that were pretty much obscured over time, covered in interstate highways or skyscrapers or subdivisions. But here, he realized, he could actually step on the exact same ground were Indians once walked, or slaves, or maybe a Civil War soldier. It was exciting, but creepy, especially in light of the two curious visitors he had involuntarily entertained in the last few days.

"Terry? Earth-to-Terry! Are you still with me?" Aunt Penny was calling to her daydreaming nephew.

He blushed. "I'm here," he said. "Just thinking."

"Well that's obvious," said his aunt. "Anything you want to share? I've done all the talking."

Terry rocked his head back and forth as if trying to make up his mind. At last he said, "Well, I doubt you want to hear this, but we had another visitor today. A girl."

Chapter twelve

bumps in the night

At first, Aunt Penny looked exasperated. Terry knew she had jumped to the wrong conclusion that he had invited some girl over to visit him. How she figured that—when he had no phone—he couldn't fathom.

"Who?" she asked suspiciously.

"Missy," Terry answered. He shrugged his shoulders. "At least that's who she said she was. She came right in the back door like old Nus Marster did. I was camped out in the big armchair in the parlor." He nodded toward the other room. "I guess I was dozing and when I opened my eyes, she was just sitting there on the ottoman in front of me—'bout scared me to death."

Aunt Penny acted confused and concerned. "What did she want? What did she say?"

Terry sighed. "She was just a little kid, about nine, I guess. Black. Dressed like...like, well, maybe slave days, pretty raggedy but clean. Had a quilt with her. She sewed on it, showed me how it had a secret pocket. Made me some tea."

"And then?" Aunt Penny demanded after Terry finished his account of the visit.

"I guess I dozed off again, and when I woke up she was gone, and you were here cooking dinner," Terry explained.

For a minute, Aunt Penny drummed her fingers on the table. Then she jumped up and checked the back door; it was locked. Without another word, she cleaned up the kitchen. Then she turned to her nephew and said, "Let's go in the other room and talk." Terry didn't like the mysterious tone in her voice.

In the parlor, Terry slumped back down into the armchair. His aunt stoked the fire, then sat on the ottoman in front of him. She picked up the plantation journal he had been reading and thumbed through it thoughtfully. Outside, through the wavery glass windows, Terry spied the full moon. He wondered which moon it was...the Wolf Moon? The Full Flower Moon? Indians had special names for each month's full moon. Once, he had tried to memorize them out of an old *Farmer's Almanac*, but he could never keep them straight.

Aunt Penny startled them both when she finally speared the silence with a nervous, cracked voice.

"Terry, there are some things I need to tell you about Pickpocket Plantation." When Terry just looked at her with quizzical blue eyes, she went on.

"You know, lowcountry Georgia and the Carolinas are sort of a unique place. They aren't exactly on the beaten path, except for the beaches in summer with tourists, Lord knows. I mean, this very land and river is where the Creek and Yamacraw Indians once lived...and died."

"Or were killed by disease or white men," Terry added. He knew his history pretty good. He recalled that sometimes, early colonists even gave the native people blankets infected with smallpox. Since they had no immunity to the disease, it often killed entire tribes. Pretty dirty pool, he thought.

His aunt nodded. "Yes. And I guess we're glad General Oglethorpe founded the city of Savannah and claimed it for the so-called New World, which one day, would be known as Georgia and America. But that just ended up bringing about some more bad stuff."

When his aunt hesitated, Terry filled in the blank: "Slavery."

Once more his aunt nodded in agreement. Outside the wind had come up and clotted cotton clouds blotted the light from the moon. Did every night have to bring a thunderstorm, Terry wondered to himself.

"Slavery," repeated Aunt Penny. "Including right here at Pickpocket...to plant and harvest the rice, and keep the plantation going. Summers were hot; the mosquitoes were as big as dinner plates. Some masters were good to their slaves, but still, they could be bought and sold, and even husbands and wives, or mothers and their children separated.

"And then there was the Civil War," she continued. "General William Tecumseh Sherman marched through here, you know. He even stayed for awhile, in one of the Savannah mansions. But out here, in the woods and forests, blood was shed as the Union and Confederate soldiers encountered each other in the river bottoms."

"Aunt Penny," Terry interrupted, as the thunder began to growl. "Are you trying to tell me something?"

She laughed. "Well, maybe...eventually. I guess I'm trying to say that there are rumors...lots of legend and lore around these parts, you know...that Pickpocket is *haunted*—but I PROMISE I don't believe it and have never seen or heard a thing."

"Never had any visitors?"

"No."

"Never felt any spooooooooooky coooooooold claammmmmy spiriiiiiiits?" Terry slowly moaned.

"Hey!" Aunt Penny said with a giggle. "You're making fun of me, aren't you? Just because I'm the scaredy cat of the century."

Terry shook his head. "No, but you don't really believe in ghosts, do you?"

Outside, the thunderstorm grumbled. Aunt Penny tucked her feet up under her and beneath an antique afghan. "Of course not," she admitted. "But, I can't always swear that I have an answer for every creak and groan I hear in this place either."

Just then, there was a loud SMACK from the kitchen. Terry and his aunt both jumped.

"Just thunder?" Terry guessed.

"Let's go seeeeeeeeee," teased his aunt to break their startled spell. "I did make desert—banana pudding. Let's have some."

Much to their chagrin, they each hesitated as they rose and marched shoulder to shoulder through the kitchen door.

"Well at least the Big Smack wasn't lightning," Terry said, heading for the kitchen table. He turned and could not understand why his aunt was standing there with her mouth hanging open, frozen in place.

Terry looked all around. "What's wrong?" he asked. "You said you made dessert."

Aunt Penny sniffed. "Yes, I did. But I left it in the refrigerator. I never put it out on the kitchen table." *But there it sat.*

Chapter thirteen

Savannah

The next morning all Terry and his aunt could think of was going to town. The evening thunderstorm had sucked all the humidity out of the air and left everything feeling fresh-washed and ghost-free. It was a gorgeous, sunny Saturday summer day.

Aunt Penny put the top down on her convertible. Terry wished he was old enough to drive, but he was happy just to escape Pickpocket for awhile and see something new and hopefully less nerve-wracking.

The winding drive down the crushed oyster shell path felt like one thing to Terry—fun. The cool breeze. The occasional hank of Spanish moss blew against his arm or neck; it tickled. Aunt Penny was laughing. The sunlight trickled like gold doubloons through the leaves and branches to land in untouched pebbles on the ground.

Terry not only realized that he was happy, but he also understood what his aunt must have seen in poor, neglected—perhaps even haunted?—Pickpocket Plantation when she first saw it. She saw not what it was, but what it had been in its glorious past, and what it might be once again in the future. Too bad unscrupulous developers, and perhaps others, were trying to trick (or maybe trick-or-treat scare) her out of keeping the place.

Suddenly, to the left of the drive, Terry spotted a large alligator just as it swished its tail and vanished in the shady undergrowth. Off to the right, a white-tailed deer darted into the woods. He hoped the two never met up. He felt a little like a wild animal himself, trapped between childhood and adulthood, not sure who was innocent friend or wily predator.

With a final crunch of tire on shell, Aunt Penny pulled out of the end of the long drive and onto the narrow gray highway that ran straight as string into downtown Historic Savannah. The Savannah River glistened like Christmas tinsel beside them. The sky was an electric blue. A few fat clouds created smoky companion friends on the water.

"So, uh, Savannah's the oldest town in Georgia, or something?" Terry began, to make conversation.

"My goodness, boy!" squealed Aunt Penny. "What are they teaching you up there in the big city of Atlanta? Don't you get tested on Georgia history? Savannah is so important in our state's history. General James Edward Oglethorpe made a beeline for this desirable bluff. He wanted to build a town here. Only there was one problem."

Terry guessed, "Uh, the Indians had already discovered that this was a pretty good place to live, themselves?"

Aunt Penny grinned. "Exacta-mundo! But old Oglethorpe was not about to give up. He recruited a woman named Mary Musgrove to help him. She was part Indian and part white, educated, a good businesswoman, and quite the diplomat herself. Best of all, she was able to translate between the Yamacraw and Oglethorpe's party."

"So did the Indians give in?" asked Terry, understanding that his aunt wanted to share the whole story.

"With a little persuasion," she said. "The native peoples moved on up the river. Oglethorpe laid out a town set in squares. It was a remarkable plan then, and when you see it, you'll see just how well it has held up."

No sooner had this been said, when they crested the sailing ship-like Talmadge Bridge and the magical town of Savannah came into full view. On the far bank of the river, the ballast stones and old brick of the former Cotton Exchange that now made up the shops and inns glistened in the morning sun.

"Just imagine Savannah's heyday, when the wharf was dotted with ships taking on cotton and rice and other goods. It must have been quite busy and exciting," said his aunt.

Terry nodded, admiring the gold-domed city hall with its large clock tower. Spires from various churches looked drawn against the sky. A red and black tugboat shoved a large freighter upriver. MELCHIOR the fantail read... Hong Kong. It sounded so exotic to him. He'd never been farther north than Kentucky. Would he ever travel the world? In truth, he couldn't imagine it.

Now off the bridge, Aunt Penny seemed to be trying to make him seasick as she swung the car around square after historic square. "Here's the Telfair Arts Center...and that's the oldest Methodist church in the nation...over there, look!, that statue is of Oglethorpe...and here's the big fountain in Forsyth Park."

Terry laughed. "I don't have to see it all at once!" But he was enjoying the ever-changing views, from the funky Paris Market shop to fortresslike stone buildings to square after leafy square filled with tourists, statues, pigeons, and flowers—endless colors of flowers. He spotted a batch of Girl Scouts in green vests waiting to cross the street.

"The Juliette Gordon Low House is here," his aunt explained. "Founder of the Girl Scouts. And wait till you see the city at night, all aglow with gaslights. You might enjoy the cemetery tours."

"They tour cemeteries?" Terry asked.

"Sure," said Aunt Penny. "They're beautiful, historic, and one tombstone after another of fascinating history, such as when the Yellow Fever passed through Savannah, killing hundreds...even the doctors trying to keep everyone alive. They put covers on the feet of the horses that pulled the funeral carriages so as not to disturb the sick and dying."

"And are there ghosts?" Terry teased.

His aunt said one word, "Whooooooooooooooooo," as she pulled into a parking place in front of a curious building that looked like a funeral home.

"And what's this place?" Terry asked.

Aunt Penny frowned. "It's where I work."

Inside the law firm of Abercorn, Holshouser, Pettigrew and Able, it was indeed quiet as a tomb. Thick, velvety carpet muffled their footsteps. Enormous portraits of ugly, old men having bad hair days hung in ornate frames on the walls, which were covered in wallpaper the color of dried blood.

"May I help you?" a high-pitched voice drawled. A tiny, gray-haired woman peered up from behind a counter made of marble and gold. "Oh, Miss Penny, it's you." She gave Terry the evil-eye as if he'd just walked in with mudcaked feet. "And this would be?"

"My nephew, Telesphore," his aunt said, slinging her arm over his shoulder. "Down from Atlanta." Terry cringed at the sound of his name said aloud.

But the little old woman, apparently upon hearing such an auspicious name, now smiled up at him with adoring acceptance. "Welllllllllllcome!" she drawled. Then she frowned. "But I'm terribly sorry about that Atlanta part," she added in a whisper, as if Terry had admitted he lived in a federal penitentiary.

Savannah is a little weird, Terry thought to himself. But things got weirder still when a gruff-looking but handsome man with silver hair and bright blue eyes stuck his head out of a door the size and thickness of a banquet table and said, "Penelope? Thank goodness! Get in here. The autopsy results are in."

Aunt Penny looked at her nephew with hesitation. With his eyes he pleaded for her not to make him sit out here in the morguelike lobby. She actually winced as she turned and headed for the closing door. Terry stuck as close to her as a small child grasping its mother's skirt when meeting a stranger.

And when they went into the large boardroom and Terry realized what he was seeing, he almost passed out.

Chapter fourteen

a is for autopsy

A naked body of a young man lay on the boardroom table. Sunlight streamed through the slats of the shutters and painted bright yellow stripes across the pale white corpse. A doctor in a white lab coat adroitly swept a sheet over the body when he saw that a child had entered the room. But the big, silver-haired man seemed to care less who was present. He whipped the sheet right back down with one hand and with the other jammed a dimmer switch on the wall upward causing a gigantic crystal chandelier to blast on with a brightness that made them all squint.

"See!" he pointed to Aunt Penny. "I told you there'd be an exit wound! Murder most foul...murder most foul," he muttered, shaking his tinsel-colored hair.

Aunt Penny cleared her throat and spoke quietly. "Was it really necessary to bring the poor boy here... and display him on the boardroom table like Thanksgiving dinner?"

It was all Terry could do not to burst out laughing that image sounded so funny to him. He actually made a peculiar noise as he stifled his undesired laugh so firmly that he felt like something might spew out his nose. Maybe it was just nerves, he thought. Everyone frowned at him then turned back to the body.

Terry looked too, realizing that the boy was really young, maybe only twenty or so. He also realized that he had never seen a dead body before. Now he felt a little nauseous. He hoped he wouldn't puke on the carpet. Or maybe in a fancy office like this he had to say *regurgitate*? Either way, he figured the old guy in charge would not appreciate anyone throwing up. Maybe he would even commit "murder most foul?"

Once more, his aunt cleared her throat. "Terry," this is Mr. Abercorn, head of the law firm. My boss."

The old man just nodded with a grunt and continued to stare at the body wearing nothing but two bullet holes to the chest.

"Telesphore is my nephew," Aunt Penny added. To Terry she seemed to stand a little taller and had the slightest hint of a smug smile.

Terry was astounded with the sudden about-face. Mr. Abercorn turned and shook his hand heartily. "Well, why didn't you say so, Penelope? Welcome, son. I wondered when we'd get to meet you." The other men smiled and nodded at him as if confirming he had just been admitted into some secret society and was now *one of them.* Terry was so speechless, he just shook back, smiled, and nodded. His aunt nodded approvingly. Now everyone was smiling and nodding—except the dead boy.

When the door cracked open and the little old lady from reception stuck her head inside and said, "The Graingers are here," all the smiling and nodding ceased just as instantly as it had begun. Curious glances were exchanged.

"Norton, pull the hearse to the side portico," Mr. Abercorn ordered. "Penelope, you and Telesphore wait on the widow's walk; I'll be up shortly. Mrs. Grace, give us ten minutes and then show the Graingers in."

"I'll serve tea," Mrs. Grace said pleasantly, as if this was an ordinary room with just ordinary living people present.

Mr. Abercorn and the doctor turned to their task. Aunt Penny took Terry by the arm and led him through the wall—a secret panel—that took them to a spiral staircase.

"Where are we going?" Terry asked as his aunt started up the staircase.

"The widow's walk," she said.

Terry followed in silence.

At the top of the spiral staircase, Terry was stunned by the small octagonal room made entirely of glass windows. By turning in a circle he felt he could see all of Savannah, and far beyond.

His aunt collapsed on the continuous row of upholstered window seats. "You have no idea," she exclaimed, as if to answer a question no one had asked.

"Seems like a pretty weird place to work," Terry commented. "Dead bodies...secret panels...and people who act like my real given name is some magical spell. And what's this room for anyway?"

"It's called a widow's walk," his aunt explained. "Once, this was one of the largest and most famous houses in Savannah. A sea captain lived here. Like many other seaman's wives, his often walked in circles here watching for his ship to sail into the harbor. Sometimes the ships came back...sometimes they didn't."

"And the dead body?" Terry asked, eager to get all the answers he could while his aunt was talking.

"His name is Jackson Johns. He's only twenty. Apparently he was out shooting lines—you know, doing surveys for property lines—when he was shot. Accidentally by deer hunters? Or on purpose by..."

"Developers," Terry finished.

Aunt Penny shook her head. "Oh, no developer would be that audacious. But the deed could be done at their request, or suggestion, or, well, I don't know. Unique property is at a premium here. It's sort of last

call for prime riverfront tracts of any significant size.
A lot is at stake."

"A lot of money," Terry guessed. "But murder? And
why an autopsy...here, of all places?"

Aunt Penny gazed out at the view. "After the sea
captain died at sea and his wife mourned herself to death,
this house was bought for a funeral home. Autopsies
were often performed in the basement. My boss has a lot
of clout in this town. If he wants to see a bullet hole up
close and personal, well, he can pull that off, just like
someone pulled off killing that poor, young man."

"Bullet *holes*," Terry corrected. "There were two
holes; I saw them. And by large tracts of land, you don't
happen to mean Pickpocket Plantation, do you? I saw
the surveyors at work when we pulled out of the drive
this morning. You could be in danger,"

"*We* could be in danger," his aunt now corrected him.

For a moment they were both silent as a grave,
deep in personal thought. Aunt Penny poured hot
water from a silver urn into a fragile-looking teacup.
From a silver box she pulled a teabag and dangled it in
the water like a marionette.

The simple act gave Terry an idea. "Aunt Penny!" he
said suddenly. "Do you think that your strange visitors
are being sent by some developer to give you—and me,
since I seem to be the one home when they come—the
creeps? You know, to scare you off. To make you sell."

His aunt looked stunned. "You'd make a good attorney, Terry!" she said. "I sure hope not. I think maybe your Nus Marster and Milly were just passing through. Old Indian trails, old paths through the forest; maybe they just passed by on their way to somewhere else."

Terry laughed, half in anger, half just nervous at not knowing the answer. "And just stop by to crack some nuts or put our dessert out?" The truth was, Terry believed that the two strange visitors were more likely to be able to pass through solid walls than to be passing by Pickpocket to say howdy. If it happened again, well, he would be out of there. No bullet holes for him; no way.

When a shiny silver orb suddenly poked up from the spiral staircase, they both gasped. The sun hit Mr. Abercorn's hair dead on. He came no further, just looked at them both and said, "Come below, Penelope, Telesphore." And then he vanished from their view like a rabbit in a rabbit hole.

A rascally rabbit, Terry thought as he followed his aunt down the stairs. Maybe very rascally.

Chapter fifteen

fort Pulaski

To make up for the rather gory surprise she had unwittingly exposed her nephew to, Aunt Penny decided to give Terry a fun tour of Savannah and take him to dinner before they went back home.

It was a great afternoon for a whirlwind tour in a convertible, and they soon forgot their troubles. First they headed out to Tybee to see the beach and the Atlantic Ocean charging ashore in wave after blue-green wave capped with a topknot of glistening spindrift. "You could almost surf today," Aunt Penny noted, thinking that she would surprise her nephew with a surfboard for Christmas.

Terry probably would have been disappointed not to get in the water, except that he knew their next stop was Fort Pulaski.

"Built by Robert E. Lee, right?" he asked his aunt.

"So you do know your history," she teased back then admitted, "You know, I was always secretly in love with Count Casimir Pulaski when I was a girl."

Terry laughed. "And why is that?"

Aunt Penny laughed too. "Just that—his name: *Count Casimir Pulaski*. I thought it sounded very romantic; still do. Thought if I ever had a boy I'd name him Casimir."

Terry groaned. "Poor little sucker! Well, at least now I've heard a name worse than Telesphore. Speaking of which, why did your boss and everyone act so freaked out when you said my name? The look on their faces...the change in their demeanor. What gives?"

Aunt Penny stopped the car at the peak of the bridge over the water to the fort. "It's a special name...from back in Pickpocket's heyday. *That* Telesphore was rather rich, from the cotton and rice and all, you know? He was one of the first clients the law firm had. Of course, that was their grandaddy's grandaddy's—or something—client. They made a lot of money off of him."

Terry looked impressed, both by the sturdy brick fort before them and by the story of his auspicious ancestor. "So he had legal dealings because he bought a lot of land, or was he part of the cotton exchange?"

Aunt Penny frowned. She chewed her lower lip. "No," she finally said. "He was a slave trader. He bought and sold slaves."

Terry felt like someone had sucker-punched him. This fact he did not want to hear. He did not want to know. He did not want it to be true. He glared at his aunt. "You didn't have to tell me that, you know."

She sighed. "I know. But that was the past; it has nothing to do with you. Georgia was one of the last states to allow slavery. The plantation owners swore they needed the cheap labor to survive."

"You mean free, prisoner labor," Terry argued.

"True," his aunt admitted. "No doubt it was horrible. The largest slave sale in Georgia was held on a racetrack in Savannah. It was pouring rain. Actually, most families were kept together, but adult parents and children, or adult brothers and sisters were often sold off to different places, probably never to see one another again. That day came to be known as The Weeping Time."

Terry felt like weeping himself. "I guess there are worst things than being an orphan," he finally said. "Like having family."

His aunt looked so devastated at his comment, Terry rushed to add, "I don't mean you, Aunt Penny, really! It's just so discouraging and depressing to learn such horrible news. I can't help it—it makes me feel guilty by association."

His aunt slowly drove the car across the rest of the bridge and up to the fort. "Let's feed our woes and sorrows to the alligator in the moat."

Chapter Sixteen

Stranger in the Woods

That night, Aunt Penny had an urgent call from the law firm: the case was back on. Her flight left at four in the morning. All this barely registered with Terry as he yawned and groaned and nodded when his aunt shook his shoulder to say she would be back as soon as possible. For him to have a good day and "be careful." The rest of his fitful sleep that night was dreams of what to "be careful" of.

Morning dawned with that now familiar distant war rumble of an early thunderstorm. It was battleship gray outdoors and low pale clouds raced one another across the sky. Terry decided not to sit around and feel sorry for himself. He got up and dressed in jeans and a long sleeve shirt; he was going exploring.

From the journal he pulled out an old plat of the plantation. It was wrinkled and faded and he wished he had a compass. He grabbed a bottle of water from the fridge and some kind of nutritious diet breakfast bar from a basket on the kitchen counter and set out.

Terry checked the plat and decided to see if he could make his way to the river and back. The sky looked ominous but the weather was not imminently threatening, so he shrugged and went on. For awhile a path seem to lead him. As limbs brushed his arms, he was glad he'd worn the long-sleeve shirt. Slapping a mosquito chowing down on the back of his neck, he wished he doused himself in repellant. A walking stick would be helpful too, he thought to himself, then said aloud. "No, a machete would be better!"

The path finally receded into overgrown undergrowth. Deadfall trees as big around as small cars...heaping snarls of Amazonian-like vines...the ever-teasing and tickling Spanish moss—all made the trek slow, then slower.

Soon he spotted a gray glint on the horizon—the Savannah River. Terry picked up his pace. He felt a sudden elation of "mission accomplished" and was mentally patting himself on his back when something—or someone—actually did grab him by the shoulder. Terry spun around in fright.

Before him stood a boy about his size, only his face was weary, sporting dark circles beneath his eyes and a wrinkled sunburn.

The boy spoke a single word, "Brother?"

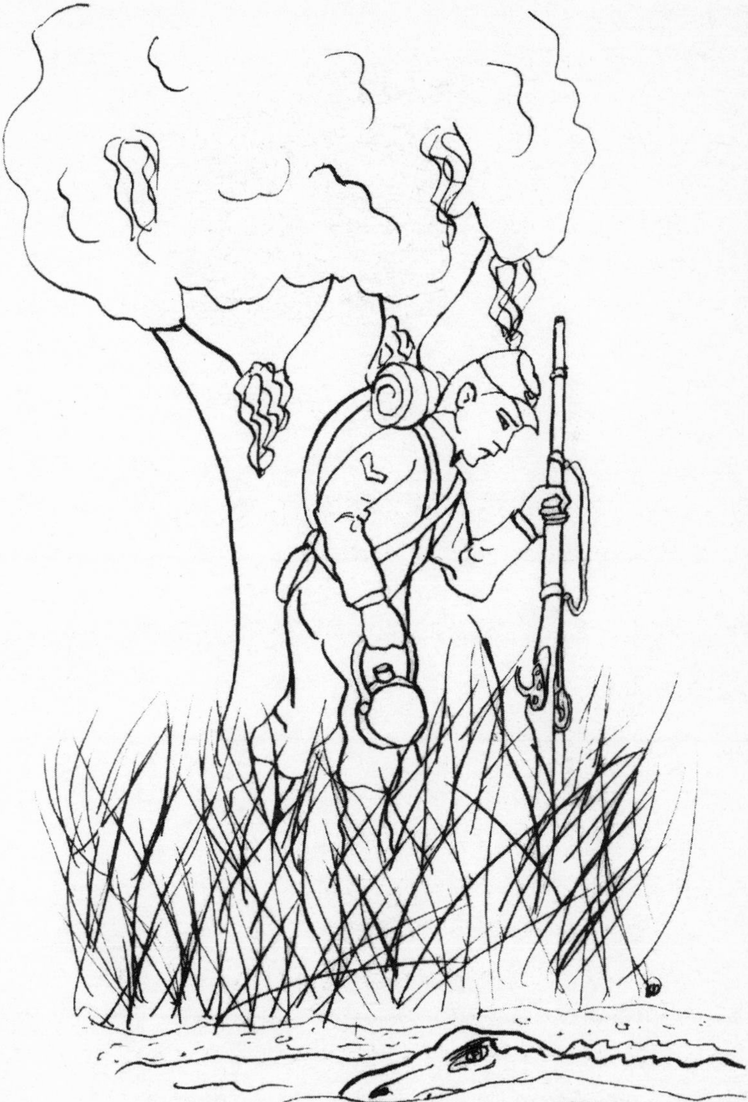

Terry jumped back. "No!" he cried, not really meaning to shout. It was then that he noticed that the boy wore a tattered Confederate uniform.

"Union?" the boy asked wearily.

"No, no," Terry said. "Who are you?"

"Mason," the boy said quietly. "Lost from my unit. No food, no water in days. No sleep. Bad dreams awake—seen too much, haystacks of amputated arms and legs up in Atlanta after the big battle. Just lookin' to go home."

Terry absolutely didn't know what to think. "Hungry?" he asked the boy.

The boy nodded. "I'd pick your pocket in a minute!" he admitted.

Terry was dumbfounded. There it was again: a stranger saying some version of *pickpocket*.

"Just messing," the boys said. "Mean you no harm. Lost my gun, lost my nerve. Just want to go home to Kentucky."

Terry pulled the water bottle from his back pocket and the breakfast bar from his shirt pocket and handed them to the boy who looked at both like they were apparitions. At last he took the water and drank it all down in one long gulp. "Funny canteen," he said. Then he tore the wrapper off the breakfast bar. "Ah, journeycake," he said with a smile.

At that moment, the heavens decided to open up and spill their contents on the two strangers. An enormous crack of thunder followed and the acrid scent of tannin and smoke as lightning struck a nearby oak. Terry turned and ran toward the river.

He didn't know what to do. There was no shelter and he knew that hiding under a tree was absolutely the wrong thing to do. Now the pouring water turned rivulets into small creeks; there seemed to be no dry land in the flooded rice paddies beneath his feet. He was scared.

But this was nothing. For Terry suddenly looked down at what sounded like thunder rumbling from the ground and found himself face to face with an enormous bull alligator! In his attempt to back up out of harm's way, Terry's heel caught a vine and he fell flat on his back in the slop of mud. As he landed hard, he heard the frightening gutteral roar that could only mean one thing.

Most people misunderstand alligators. They are wild, very wild, and they will attack you. They lounge on the ground, sprawled like lazy lizards, but they are watching, waiting. An alligator is patient; his survival depends on it.

When an alligator stands up on its legs, it is tall; most people don't realize this. It also does not lumber along but can actually run at a fast speed for a short distance. It almost always gets its prey. Usually, it pulls you underwater and twists you back and forth until you drown. Then it stores you beneath a riverbank until it is ready to eat. Generally, no one ever knows what happened to "Old Joe" who disappeared one day. "Nobody ever saw him again."

Terry was thinking these things as he waited in a slow motion daze, for he was truly unable to move. Suddenly, he felt something grasp his ankle. He said a prayer. He cried out, but only a little. Hoisting himself up on one elbow at last, he peered through the rain to see that the boy had him by the ankle with one arm, as he slugged at the big gator's nose with a tree limb with the other. "Get up, brother!" he cried. "Run!"

Somehow Terry did what he was told. He scrambled to his knees then stumbled to his feet and thrashed his way through the forest. Then he froze and turned and ran back to find the boy, to help him. Neither he nor the gator were anywhere to be seen.

Chapter Seventeen

journeycake

"I've given my notice," Aunt Penny said, upon her return. "The firm said I can come back anytime I want to, but I just feel like I need to do something different right now." They sat on the porch.

Terry was not as surprised as he thought he might have been, but he was disappointed to see his aunt give up on her dreams. "Gonna get married? Have kids?"

Aunt Penny blushed and laughed. "Not get married, probably. Have kids definitely—two, a boy and a girl."

Terry didn't know what to say. He had his own surprise to share. "I think I want to be a lawyer," he said. "I want to fight people who get in the way of other people's dreams."

His aunt looked quite taken aback. "Congratulations! I *think*? Hope I haven't been a bad influence on you this summer."

Terry shook his head. "No. I just don't think people should be able to...to...*pickpocket*...other people's dreams. People like shady developers, you know? Or, in the past, slave traders."

Aunt Penny shook her head sadly back and forth. "Oh, I agree, believe me." Then she surprised him by adding. "Terry, the reason the lawyers admired you so was because the Telesphore they knew gave up slavery after The Weeping Time. He fought to have it abolished. He became a lawyer himself and did a lot of *pro bono* work. It's even said that Pickpocket Plantation was part of the Underground Railroad, a stopping place for slaves on their way north to freedom. He helped them. He lived to be 100 and was much admired. In fact, he helped start the local Boy's Home. You can be proud of your past."

Terry was stunned. "Why didn't you tell me this the other day?" He was almost angry.

His aunt looked a little stern. "I wanted you to *think,* Terry. You can be what you want to be; the past is not about you, the future is. Besides," she added with a grin, "people try to trip lawyers up...you gotta be prepared for that!"

They sat there uncomfortably, neither really wanting the summer to be over.

"I guess I'll pack so I can go back to the Home," Terry said.

His aunt slapped her knees. "Well, speaking of the Home, that's where I plan to get my kids. I've put in the paperwork to adopt a seven-year-old girl named Liza."

Terry was stunned. "Wow," he said. "I guess that's not what I thought you meant when you said you were gonna have some kids. That's cool, real cool. Liza's a lucky girl," he said and meant it. *Adoption*. Every Home kid's dream.

"What about the boy?"

Aunt Penny laughed. When Terry looked puzzled, she said. "It's you, Terry, who else? If you'll let me."

Terry had never been so surprised in his life. Neither gators nor ghosts could have shocked him more. He thought he might cry. "Are you serious, Aunt Penny?"

She was crying and could only nod. Finally she squeaked out, "The papers are already in the works...I'm a lawyer, you know."

"Uh, I don't know what to say," Terry confessed. "That's great. I mean really, really great. Thanks." He thought his words sounded stupid as if she had just given him a bag of chips or something, not volunteered of her own free will to have him as her son. Finally he stammered, "I can't wait to get back to the Home and tell everyone."

Aunt Penny scratched her head and smiled. "Terry," she said softly. "You *are* home...son."

Now Terry was speechless. He looked around the room searching for some meaning to her comment. "But I thought you were going to sell Pickpocket. It's going to cost you a FORTUNE to fix the place up!"

His aunt surprised him by gritting her teeth and growling like a wild animal. "No way!" she said. "I'll never sell the house and the land around it. I'm selling 500 acres along the river down to the highway to a developer whom I know will be responsible with the land. That will give us the money to fix this place up. Make it a real home, ghosts and all! You can finish school here, then maybe go to law school in Charleston? What do you say?"

What Terry was thinking is that, miraculously, dreams can come true in the most unexpected ways. What he said was, "Aunt Penny...Mom?...this is all pretty darn sudden. Pretty darn scary." And then he laughed. "And, really, pretty darn wonderful."

Postlogue

On Pickpocket Plantation, the lazy leaves slowly considered changing their color. Alligators and turtles sunned in the tidewater creeks. Birds *too-weeted* in the ancient oaks. Along an old Indian path, an ageless black man picked black walnuts from the ground. In the shady nooks and crannies of the roots of a wild sycamore tree a small girl hummed and quilted. Across the river, a boy in uniform checked the tide level with a stick to gauge when he might be able to make his way back across. Alongside the highway, an orange-vested work crew shot survey lines in anticipation of the next big river tract to be developed. In the parlor, a woman took a few minutes to look at wallpaper swatches, while at the table, a boy pulled out a new leather journal and opened it to make his first entry.

the End

about the
Series Creator

Carole Marsh is an author and publisher who has written many works of fiction and non-fiction for young readers. She travels throughout the United States and around the world to research her books. In 1979 Carole Marsh was named Communicator of the Year for her corporate communications work with major national and international corporations.

Marsh is the founder and CEO of Gallopade International, established in 1979. Today, Gallopade International is widely recognized as a leading source of educational materials for every state and many countries. Marsh and Gallopade were recipients of the 2002 Teachers' Choice Award. Marsh has written more than 25 Carole Marsh Mysteries™. Years ago, her children, Michele and Michael, were the original characters in her mystery books. Today, they continue the Carole Marsh Books tradition by working at Gallopade. By adding grandchildren Grant and Christina as new mystery characters, she has continued the tradition for a third generation.

Ms. Marsh welcomes correspondence from her readers. You can e-mail her at carole@gallopade.com, visit the carolemarshmysteries.com website, or write to her in care of Gallopade International, P.O. Box 2779, Peachtree City, Georgia, 30269 USA.

built-in book Club
talk about it!

Questions for Discussion

1. If you look at old plats of real plantation lands on the Savannah River, you will see names like Graveyard Road and Dead Man's Point. How might such places have gotten their names?

2. Eli Whitney invented the cotton gin while staying at a coastal plantation. How might such an invention have changed the desperate need for slave labor?

3. Rice was a very labor-intensive and dangerous crop to grow. You had to flood the fields which meant that there was often a great deal of deep water to work in, and most workers had never learned to swim. There were floodgates, water moccasins, alligators, thunderstorms, sharp tools, great heat, masses of mosquitoes (which often brought disease), and long hours. How do you think these working conditions affected the slave labor, as well as the plantation owners?

4. Mary Musgrove is one of the most unusual women in Georgia history. She was young, an Indian, and educated. She served not only as an interpreter but a diplomat between Gen. Oglethorpe and the Yamacraw. She opened a successful trading post. At one point, she was the largest landowner in the state. How do these facts jive with the general perception of "Indian woman" of that era?

5. While most people think of slave owners as mean and cruel, the truth is that some plantation owners were very concerned about the health and wellbeing of their slaves. They might try to teach them to read, have a medical clinic at the plantation to treat them for sickness and wounds, and even encourage them to hold church services. How do such facts affect, if they do, your ideas about slave owners of the past?

6. Which parts of this book do you think the author made up? Which parts do you believe are true?

built-in book Club

bring it to life!

Activities to Do

1. Write a Last Will and Testament; use a real pen and bottled ink and write in on parchment, or parchmentlike paper.

2. Create a fictional journal from an old plantation; write entries as if you were the owner; pick a certain period of time, such as a planting season, or during a hurricane.

3. Draw a plat of an imaginary plantation; give it a name; draw in all the boundaries, all geographical places, and buildings and structures.

4. Create a classroom "recipe box" and have each student write one "recipe" for an old cure or medication or medicinal tea to add to the box; you can turn the info into a booklet, as well.

5. Research and find recipes for old colonial recipes such as cornpone, journeycake, rice pudding, or other. Make some of the recipes and do a taste test!

6. Host a class quilting bee. Each student bring a scrap of fabric and draw on it something about Pickpocket Plantation. Sew the squares together; add a backing of old sheet, then stuff the quilt with cotton batting; finish by quilting through the fabric and adding an edge all around.

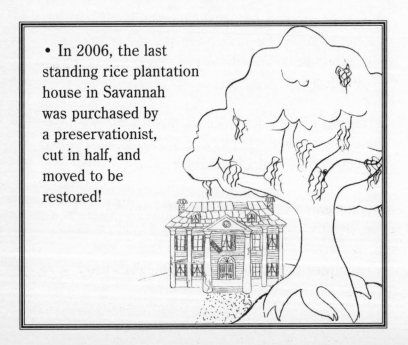

• In 2006, the last standing rice plantation house in Savannah was purchased by a preservationist, cut in half, and moved to be restored!

Pretty darn Scary
glossary

apparition: a ghost or ghostlike figure

archipelago: a string of things, such as islands

autopsy: an official medical exam of a dead body to determine the cause of death, especially in the event of suspected foul play

chagrin: surprise or dismay

eclectic: an odd assortment of things that don't quite match or go together

pro bono: work a lawyer does for free for those who can't afford to pay; Latin, meaning for (pro) good (bono)

serendipity: a sudden, unexpected surprise or coincidence

status quo: Latin for keeping things the same as they are

Pretty darn Scary
Scavenger hunt

Check off this list by finding the items in the book, or by visiting a real-life plantation!

__1. A parlor

__2. A Kitchen House

__3. An old journal

__4. A handmade quilt's counterpane

__5. An old Indian remedy

__6. A "wavery" pane of old glass

__7. A pair of andirons

__8. A journeycake

__9. A plat

__10. A Last Will and Testament

tech
Connects...
...and more!

Useful Websites to Visit

On The Weeping Time...
www.pbs.org/wgbh/aia/part4/4p2918/html

On Fort Pulaski...
www.nps.gov/fopu

On Native American and other history in the
Savannah area...
www.massieschool.com

More resources

Tombee, Portrait of a Cotton Planter by Theodore
Rosengarten

*Savannah River Plantations: Photographs from the Collection
of The Georgia Historical Society* by Frank T. Wheeler

enjoy this excerpt from...

The Secret of

SKULLCRACKER SWAMP

by Carole Marsh

#2

CHAPTER ONE

SKULLCRACKER SWAMP

Tabby hunkered down in the canvas tent, squatted, squirmed, and performed other gyrations to pull on her white cut-off jeans and a brown tee shirt with boot prints on the back that read: TAKE A HIKE.

Sure, she thought, as she squiggled into the jeans and tried to zip them while hovering on her knees and bending backwards; the tent was a small one-person pop-up job. *Sure, hike in a swamp; get eaten alive.*

Tabby was a city girl. She had grown up in Atlanta, Georgia—the City of the South, the Phoenix that Rose from the Ashes. She had lived with her grandmother in a modern condo practically at the crossroads of the famous Peachtree Street and Ponce de Leon Avenue. The fabulous Fox Theater was nearby, a Persian gem of a castle where her grandmother took her to Broadway performances, ballets, and to see *Gone With the Wind* on the giant movie screen. The marquee out front, lit up in colorful neon lights, actually gave her goosebumps.

But the goosebumps she got in this swamp was a different matter entirely. She was living with her dad this summer. He was a Swampmaster, or something like that, she'd call it. It was worse than being the daughter of Crocodile Dundee or Animal Planet's Alligator Guy, or whatever he called himself.

Actually, her father was a professor and famous for his environmental efforts regarding swamps and saving them from destruction. Tabby just wished he'd do it without her. She loved him, but really, was this anyway to spend a summer? Hunkered down in a squat, smelly tent? Swatting mosquitoes the size of saucers? Sweating to beat the band? No friends except frogs...and she did NOT like frogs. Nothing to do but wait for Dad to get back from that day's journey into the hinterlands of the swamp to do who-knew-what?

"Have fun!" he'd say merrily, as he tramped off. "Explore! I'll be back at sunset and we'll have a feast!"

Of course, Tabby was afraid to explore. She was not having any fun at all. And her father's idea of a feast was roast possum or some other critter he'd nabbed in the swamp.

It was a nightmare, she thought. This summer was a nightmare. Not only did she fear that she would not survive it, she was not even sure that she wanted to survive it. It didn't help that the never-ending swath of weeds and water which surrounded them was nicknamed Skullcracker Swamp by her father and his long-time swamp friend, Mable. It was pretty darn scary here.

Suddenly, Tabby heard a creaking, the snap of twigs, the heavy fall of footstep. Trembling, she unzipped the tent a few inches and poked her head out. It was her Dad, coming ashore in his little boat, traipsing through the wet grass toward her like Indiana Bones, as she had secretly nicknamed him.

"Hey," he greeted her with a grin. "Look what I brought for dinner!"

Tabby's father held up one fat, dead armadillo. Tabby pulled her head back inside the tent, rezipped it angrily, and fell down onto a rough tarp.

She began to cry.